Monty and the Slobbernosserus

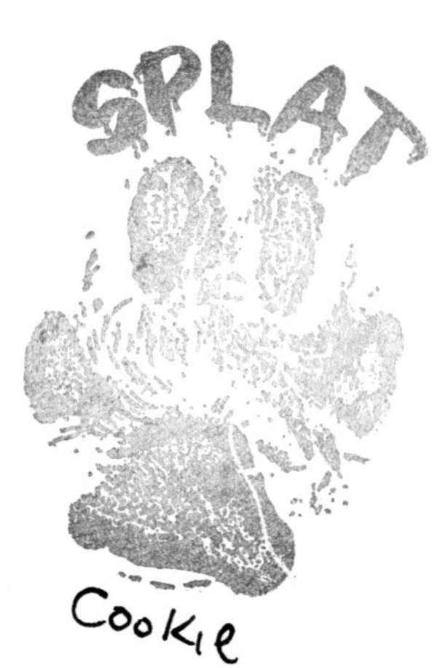

M.T Sanders

Illustrations by Rebecca Sharp

To, Macen and Carson
Love from
Monty & Cookie

First Edition published 2017 by 2QT Limited (Publishing) Settle, North Yorkshire BD24 9RH United Kingdom

Illustrations by Rebecca Sharp

Printed in Great Britain by Lightning Source

A CIP catalogue record for this book is available from the British Library

ISBN 978-1-912014-79-8

To Dianne Barrass for letting Cookie come into our lives.
We will forever be grateful to you for our beautiful girl.

To my Grandchildren Charlie, Isobel, Jack, Katie, Millie,
Oliver, Pippa (Pipsqueak) and Thomas. You are the inspiration
- Mark

Thanks to all of the hoomans who bought the first book. I realise
you'll be hoping it gets better but I'm sorry Dad is still involved
- Monty

To my Father, Brother, Sister and Dawn
you mean the world to me and more.
My best friend Genna for everything you are and do.
Love with all my heart

- Bekki xx

I never wanted a sister, that's for sure. My life was very peaceful and I liked it that way. The Spangles had stopped teasing me and, now that I was fully-grown, if they were mean I could just sit on them ... splat!

One day, and without warning, she arrived ... my new sister. Mum and Dad came in to the house clutching a smallish, brown and very hairy baby Newfydoof.

Cookie was okay at first because she slept a lot. But she began to grow and, as she did, she got naughtier and naughtier ... and very slobbery.

She would bounce on me when I was sleeping or hang onto my tail when I walked past. It was worse for the Spangles because they had two dangly ears for Cookie to chase – and that soon became her favourite game.

One day Mum and Dad had to go out but before they left they said, 'You look after your sister, Monty. You are the eldest so we're depending on you.'

I looked across at Cookie, who was pretending to be asleep, and I'm sure that was a grin on her face.

All was quiet until I heard the postyman at the door. I had to go and bark at him and jump up at the door because this is my main job during the day.

Cookie was in the back garden chewing Spangle ears when she saw the postyman going back up the street. She got very excited, thinking that this could be someone new to play with. She jumped at the back gate, which wasn't shut properly, and ... it opened.

My massive hairy sister was now free to go and explore. The postyman had just got to the top of the street ... with Cookie in hot pursuit. I knew that I had to go as well – I had to stop her causing trouble.

By the time she reached the postyman,
Cookie was panting with excitement.
Two huge, dangly strings of drool
were hanging from her mouth.
As the postyman turned, he
saw her just as she was
about to jump on him.
He screamed, 'Aaaghh!
Get this slobbery
monster off me!'

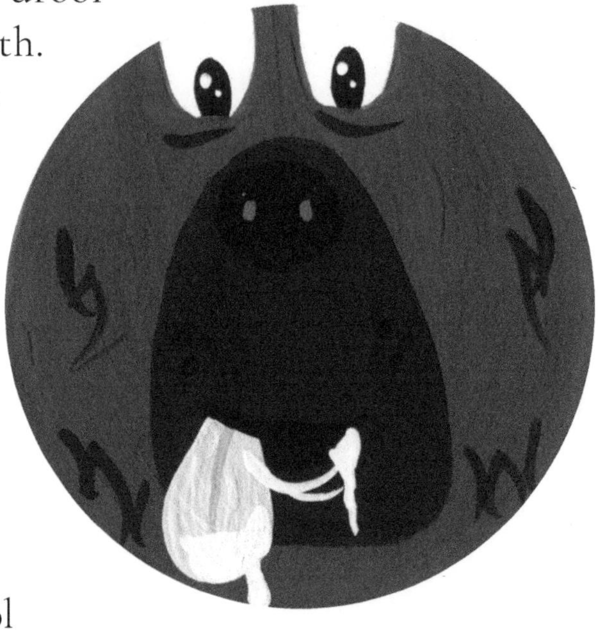

Cookie saw the postyman
and thought he'd like to play.

Big kisses made of sticky drool
is the Newfydoofy way,

As she pinned him down to love him,
it made him curse and cuss,

He wasn't happy being cuddled by the Slobbernosserus.

A French Puddle called Maurice was out for a walk when he saw what was happening and heard a hooman screaming, 'Aaaghh! A Slobbernosserus!'

Maurice's hearing wasn't too good.

Not knowing what one of these creatures was, he stopped and looked ... but then it spotted him and began to run towards him.

When I got around the corner, Cookie was already giving Maurice kisses. All I could hear was,
'Please don't eat me! Save me
from the Slobbernosserus!'

Poor Maurice saw the
Slobbernosserus running up the street,

He thought he was a tasty snack the beast would like to eat.

He couldn't get away, there was nothing he could do,

But he didn't get devoured just got covered in her goo.

I had no time to rest in my pursuit because Cookie had already left and was saying hello to a group of mini-hoomans outside the learning zoo.

The teacher called them into class and they ran happily through the playground, hand in hand. It wasn't that they were being friendly ... they were all stuck together!

The mini-hoomans screamed with joy seeing Cookie on her way,

They wanted just to fuss her and let her join in their play.

But when they went back into school after their Newfy fuss,

They'd been firmly glued together by the Slobbernosserus.

School

I was out of breath by the time I got to the learning zoo and saw Cookie's tail disappearing around the corner.

Dave was the school cat and nothing really bothered him. As he went on his morning stroll around the school grounds, he heard the excitement and decided to come over and see what a Slobbernosserus was all about.

As they came face to face, Dave gave Cookie's head a friendly pat. Cookie didn't understand gentle and her own tap, which landed on poor Dave's head, was a very long tap. It actually squashed Dave down and pinned him to the floor.

This is fun, thought Cookie, and she kissed Dave excitedly as he struggled to get free. When she finally let go, Dave looked like a jack-in-the-box flying out of a bowl of jelly. As soon as he hit the floor, he was gone...

Dave wanted to get closer to this creature near the school.
Nothing ever bothered him because he was real cool.
But the Slobbernosserus was different from anything before,
That's just what he was thinking as it pinned him to the floor...

Tails were still all I was seeing as I tried to catch up with Cookie. This time it was Dave's going one way and my naughty sister's heading the other. As I went around the corner, Cookie stopped for a rest.

'This is my chance to catch up,' I thought.

As Cookie stopped on the tree-lined path, Stan the squirrel was on his way back to his dray with the nuts he'd collected. They didn't spot each other. Then suddenly Cookie, who was really panting now with all the excitement, gave a massive shake to try and get rid of the drool hanging almost to the floor.

Unluckily for Stan, he saw the flying Newfy gunk too late...

Cookie carried on with her exploring, unaware of what she had done. By the time I got there, all I saw was Stan, chattering angrily and hanging from a branch.

Stan never thought today would come to such a sticky end.

This Slobbernosserus was dangerous, it was no squirrel's friend

He didn't see the Newfygoo as Cookie made it sail,

But it left him hanging upside down, suspended by his tail.

By this time Cookie was starting to get hungry and thought it was time to head home, so she headed back to cross the main road. As she got nearer to the road, she saw a hooman dressed all over in bright yellow and waving a big metal lollipop in her hand.

The lady was looking the other way, so Cookie thought it would be fun to surprise her. She leapt on the lady from behind and her big paws went around her neck. Thinking she was being attacked by a bear, the lady screamed and the lollipop flew into the air.

I watched from a distance as the sign stuck into the road and all the cars came to a halt.

The lady at the crossing was standing unaware

that the Slobbernosserus was coming and she got a massive scare.

'Stop, Children!' said her gooey sign, stuck in the busy road,

And now there was a massive jam where once the traffic flowed.

SERVICES
SCHOOL
HGV
SVY723H
JPD 692F
STOP

A reporter at the *Wigwam Bugle* saw Cookie bouncing on the crossing lady. He quickly grabbed his camera, but Cookie had disappeared around the corner. He phoned his newspaper. 'You're never going to guess what I've just seen.'

I was right behind Cookie and caught up with her at the top of the street. 'Quick,' I said. 'We need to get back because if Mum and Dad see this, you're in big trouble ... and so am I!'

With that, we both ran as fast as we could towards the house. I kept looking nervously over my shoulder.

We got back into the house just as Mum and Dad pulled up in the car. Funnily enough, they had been delayed by a big traffic jam. When they came into the house they found us both lying calmly in the hall. 'Good dogs,' said Dad. 'Having a nice quiet day?'

We heard no more until a few days later when Dad was reading the newspaper. 'Look at this, love,' he said to Mum. 'This must have been what held us up the other day'.

He held up the paper and there was a headline: *Mysterious Slobbernosserus Causes Chaos in Wigwam.*

I looked across at Cookie and she looked at me – and I'm sure I saw that grin again.

There was panic in the town, there was talk about a creature.

It had drooling fangs and orange legs – the paper did a feature.

No one ever worked it out, nobody knew but us,

And we still keep the secret of the Slobbernosserus.

Also available in all good bookshops
and at www.montydogge.com

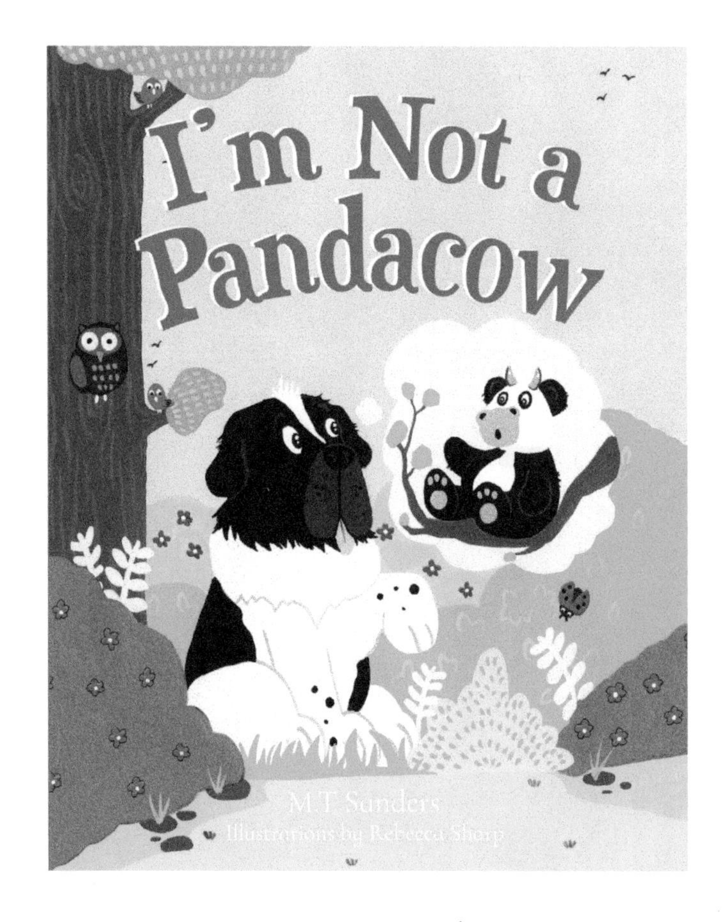

By M.T Sanders
with Illustrations by Rebecca Sharp
ISBN 978-1-912014-7-3

Lightning Source UK Ltd.
Milton Keynes UK
UKHW052219270519
343397UK00002B/7/P

9 781912 014798